THE WHITE Elephant

Also by Sid Fleischman

The Whipping Boy

The Scarebird

The Ghost in the Noonday Sun

The Midnight Horse

McBroom's Wonderful One-Acre Farm

Here Comes McBroom!

Mr. Mysterious & Company

Chancy and the Grand Rascal

The Ghost on Saturday Night

Jim Ugly

The 13th Floor

The Abracadabra Kid

Bandit's Moon

A Carnival of Animals

Bo and Mzzz Mad

Disappearing Act

The Giant Rat of Sumatra

Escape! The Story of The Great Houdini

THE WHITE
Elephant

by
SID FLEISCHMAN

illustrations by
ROBERT MCGUIRE

GREENWILLOW BOOKS
An Imprint of HarperCollinsPublishers

The White Elephant

Copyright © 2006 by Sid Fleischman, Inc.

All rights reserved. No part of this book may be used or reproduced in any manner whatsoever without written permission except in the case of brief quotations embodied in critical articles and reviews. Printed in the United States of America. For information address HarperCollins Children's Books, a division of HarperCollins Publishers, 1350 Avenue of the Americas, New York, NY 10019. www.harpercollinschildrens.com

The text of this book is set in 14-point Granjon.

Library of Congress Cataloging-in-Publication Data
Fleischman, Sid, (date).
The white elephant / by Sid Fleischman.
    p. cm.
"Greenwillow Books."
Summary: In old Siam, young elephant trainer Run-Run and his old charge, Walking Mountain, must deal with the curse of a sacred white elephant.
ISBN-10: 0-06-113136-9 (trade bdg.) ISBN-13: 978-0-06-113136-3 (trade bdg.)
ISBN-10: 0-06-113137-7 (lib. bdg.) ISBN-13: 978-0-06-113137-0 (lib. bdg.)
[1. Elephants—Fiction. 2. Thailand—History—To 1782—Fiction.] I. Title.
PZ7.F5992Wk 2006 [Fic]—dc22 2005046793

First Edition 10 9 8 7 6 5 4 3 2 1

GREENWILLOW BOOKS

For Sarah Conley,
girl of the elephants

Contents

THE WHITE
Elephant

Run-Run and the tall elephant turned up the road leading to his hillside village.

A Smile FOR Run-Run

There, in old Siam, do you see the boy with dirty ears sitting as proud as a prince on the tall old elephant? Oh, how those two love each other! The boy, whose name is Run-Run, sometimes sleeps between the elephant's front legs, safe from the world.

But what a terrible mischief the elephant got that boy into!

It happened on a day like today, hot as an oven with its doors flung open.

They were returning from clearing the tangled stumps of aged jackfruit trees for the new mango plantation over on the hillside. The tall elephant would get a stump between his great yellow tusks and shove with his padded forehead. Out came the stump, squealing like a bad tooth.

"Walking Mountain!" the boy shouted with a smile, for that was the elephant's name. "A morning's work under this sun is enough, big brother! Your old bones ache, eh? Come, let us have a bath, great Walking Mountain."

Half a century old, was Run-Run's elephant, with his final set of teeth! Walking Mountain had carried the boy's father on his neck, and his father's father. Brave mahouts, they commanded elephants many times their size. Mahouts had been Run-Run's tutors. Now, only half grown, he, too, was a mahout, with his father's colored headdress packed away under his grandfather's porcelain amulet.

But how many years could Walking Mountain remain on

his legs? One day he would lie down, lame and toothless, and refuse to get up.

In the river, Run-Run washed his ears and the red dust out of his hair, as if to avoid a scolding from his mother. He had been barely eight when she was mauled by a tiger. They say she'd fought the wild creature, even biting off his ear. Someday, Run-Run would meet that great cat, that awful, one-eared beast, and then, watch out, murderer!

"But, where are you, tiger?" Run-Run sometimes muttered. "Afraid to venture out of the jungle and show your ugly eyes around here, eh?"

Tight-lipped, he replied to his own question. "Dreamer! And what if he has been shot dead by a hunter? Aye, dead and eaten by flies!

"I bless the flies," he added.

Now he gave his head a toss, and his long and black hair wrapped itself around his neck like a wet towel.

Run-Run and the tall elephant turned up the road leading

to his hillside village. Tucked far below the hazy teak mountains to the north, shady Chattershee would be hard for anyone in the kingdom of Siam to find. No one except the pariah dogs who could be heard barking as Walking Mountain shuffled by; no one except the fruit bats, the wild green parrots, and a tiger or two.

Summer was brief with airless days, bringing heat as fiery as dragon's breath. Dust rose in clouds like gnats.

Nevertheless, Run-Run had smiles for the world. The coins jingling in the pouch around his neck would buy grain for his elephant. Fresh hay, too, brought to the plantation by bullock carts from he knew not where. He'd slap his noisy coins on the counter and pick out a treat of spindly sugarcanes for his tall friend. And why not a fat, juicy piece of cane for himself, Run-Run, to chew?

Oh, how that great walking mountain could eat! Two hundred pounds a day. Three hundred! Hardly a blade of grass was left at the edges of the plowed fields to dine upon.

For miles around, plantation elephants had browsed the tree branches up beyond reach. But being so tall, Walking Mountain could stand on his hind legs and stretch himself to amazing length to search out a high mango or luscious fruits dangling on the wild fig trees.

"Elephant boy!" called out the beekeeper, old Bangrak. He sat in the breathless shade of a flame tree. "Look! Here is a watermelon I grew for you in exchange."

"A thousand blessings!" exclaimed Run-Run, running his tongue around his lips. "In exchange for what, sir?"

"My wind chimes haven't struck a note in weeks. If I breathe more dust, I'll spit mud bricks! Give this road a river splash, eh?"

"Two watermelons," said Run-Run, for bargaining was as natural to him as breathing. Sometimes a trade in river water arose out of the choking April dust. He would be sorry to see the monsoon rains come and put his splendid business at an end.

"Did you say two melons?"

"Indeed, sir."

"Thief!" The old man wagged a dried hand in front of his face as if to clear a swirl of dust.

Said Run-Run, "I am ashamed of myself! Nevertheless, a melon for Walking Mountain. Another for me."

"Prince of rascals!"

"Two watermelons, large and sweet, or good-bye, friend of my father," the elephant boy replied.

Like an actor playing a part he loved, old Bangrak gave a snarl in disgust, but with a smile tucked into his white beard. For him, too, bargaining was a skill and an entertainment to be admired. It was relentless bargaining that had allowed him to send his son off to the city and to school. It was rumored that the boy could already read and write. Such an achievement was the talk of the village.

"Two watermelons are too much!" Old Bangrak insisted.

"Three would be more to my liking," said Run-Run.

"Scamp! Two! It is agreed!"

Run-Run called to his elephant. "Give an ear, Walking Mountain! To the river, magnificent one!"

Run-Run climbed to the elephant's neck and took his familiar place. With a light touch of the bull hook left to him by his father, Run-Run turned the elephant toward the river below. "Go!"

There Walking Mountain filled his long trunk with water. He hardly needed a command from Run-Run to lumber back to the village and spray. After several trips the red dust was settling over the road like a fresh coat of paint.

The village children had gathered to watch and now yelled out.

"Elephant Boy! How about a splash for us, eh?"

Walking Mountain gave the children a cloudburst of rain. They screamed and pranced about with delight. Between the elephant's huge flapping ears, Run-Run sat smiling, with his arms folded like a young monarch. The pariah dogs came trotting over to have a look. Then the elephant and his young mahout returned to the river for another trunkful of water.

That was a mistake. How was Run-Run to know?

CHAPTER 2

"It is me, the careless mahout, who deserves to be shot!"

Run-Run AND THE Terrible Mischief

Moments later, one of the king's many princes—the one called Noi the Idle—came thundering through the red dust on his gaily decorated elephant. Leading a small hunting party, he rode standing up in a wicker basket, a howdah. Strapped to the back of his elephant like a great saddle, the elaborately woven wicker had the appearance of a swaying garden gazebo.

But no! Wait! Could this be the very instant Walking Mountain's trunk was full of river water—his trunk raised high in the air?

With a roar, the tall elephant emptied his trunk. Water and a small fish or two sprayed out as if shot from a cannon. A typhoon of water splashed over the prince.

Under a golden headdress rising to a point, like a temple spire, Prince Noi erupted. He rumbled. He roared. He slapped off a tiny river eel tangled among the medals rattling like coins on his chest.

"Shoot that insolent elephant!" he commanded.

Run-Run awoke from his surprise. "Ten thousand sorrows, excellent lordship!" he cried out. "We did not see your beloved shadow through the dust! It is that stupid Run-Run who is at fault. Ten thousand apologies! It is me, the careless mahout, who deserves to be shot!"

"You?" The prince paused, pinching water off his great hawk's nose. A dark fury, like a storm approaching, advanced across his face. "So! Shall I squash your worthless life, instead? Shall I use you for target practice?"

"Ten thousand—"

"Spare me your blessings, elephant brat!"

"As you command."

Bemused by a stroke of an idea, Prince Noi threw his shoulders back and burst into a startling laugh. "No! You must set an example! A prince is not to be made a fool! I shall send a gift to punish you!"

Run-Run couldn't hold back a baffled gaze. Did he hear right? "A gift, my lord?"

He allowed a hopeful smile to escape. Could Prince Noi be kinder than his reputation?

"A gift can be sharper than a rifle ball between your scrawny ribs! You will see! Yes, yes, a gift to curse you and to curse your father and to curse your children for generations to come!"

The smile slid off Run-Run's face. Bowing his head, he said, "Great prince, surely you are too generous. Would you go to so much bother for a lowly dung beetle like Run-Run?

A buzzing summer fly? A flick with the back of your hand will be sufficient."

"Shall I take advice from an elephant brat?"

The prince gave a signal to his mahout, and the royal elephant swung away. Others in the party followed.

Run-Run let out a great sigh. He gave his old elephant a light tap and turned back for the two watermelons waiting under the flame tree.

"What gift could be sharper than a bullet?" he asked old Bangrak. "And a curse, too?"

"He is vengeful and hot tempered, our idle prince," replied the village elder. "Let us wait and see."

Run-Run rolled a watermelon toward Walking Mountain's feet. "One for you and one for me," he said. "Eat, big brother!"

CHAPTER 3

"Full of himself, is that white elephant!"

The Curse ON Run-Run

Run-Run watched Walking Mountain enjoy his watermelon. The elephant stomped a foot, as if cracking open a nut. He curled the tip of his trunk around the random hunks of melon. Within moments, there was nothing left but a dark stain in the dust.

Run-Run, eating his own melon, kept throwing Walking Mountain the rinds. A piece or two he tossed to the pariah dogs, who always seemed to expect their share of village scraps.

He recalled the dogs barking at the district doctor. The foreigner had come to ease his mother as she lay in pain after the tiger mauling. Run-Run had never before seen such a fellow, with papers to show how clever he was. How did one become a doctor? It would take baskets and baskets of coins, wouldn't it? Only wondering, Run-Run thought, finishing the melon.

Early the next morning a mist hung over the river when Run-Run called out a command and touched a rear leg. "Up, beloved!" The elephant raised the foot, and the boy set to work filing the animal's tender toenails and leveling the pads of his feet. He had learned in earliest childhood that a mahout's first duty was to care for his elephant's feet. A thorn, a split nail might let sickness and death slip in. In his young life, Run-Run had seen many a mahout unable to keep his footsore animal alive.

Finishing with Walking Mountain's feet, Run-Run gave the animal a final pat. "How about a mud bath, eh?"

The boy rode the swaying elephant down the path to the river's edge and the heavily shaded mud shallows. Jumping to the ground, he turned Walking Mountain loose to roll about in the wallow.

Run-Run helped cover the animal's hide, for a plastering of mud protected the skin from ticks and mosquitoes and sunburn. Soon the young mahout and his old elephant would be ready for the day's work.

But who was coming? With his arms muddy to the elbows, he looked up.

Three girls from the village came running down to tell Run-Run that his gift from the prince had arrived.

"What is it?" he asked.

"You'll see! White as a cloud!"

Run-Run began washing the mud off his arms. A gift that was also a curse? How could that be? He gave the girls a bold smile. Why let the world know he was worried and even frightened?

At Run-Run's command, Walking Mountain kneeled. Run-Run scampered like a mouse from wrinkled knee to hairy neck and seated himself. The two quickly followed the hill path to the village.

There stood the prince's gift, giving a flap of its great ears. It was an elephant. Run-Run gazed at it, wide-eyed with amazement and quick admiration. Not just a common elephant—no. A white elephant! Yes, white as a cloud.

The animal looked young, perhaps only on its second set of teeth. It was slim and fit, with tusks as sharp as crescent moons. His eyes glistened like princely pearls, shaded by long, rusty eyelashes. He peered at Run-Run and then dismissed the boy without further interest.

"Doesn't he give himself airs!" the boy muttered to Walking Mountain. "Full of himself, is that white elephant! And look at that tail."

The beast's tail ended with a white tuft of hair, afloat like a fine silk handkerchief, to brush off flies, as it was doing now.

The palace mahout, wearing a tight red jacket, handed Run-Run an *ankus* to prod the elephant. Such an ankus! Engraved with vines that the village boy had never seen before in the jungle. Was it silver?

Said the mahout, his words giving off sparks as if sharpened at a grinding wheel, "You! He's yours! Bathe him! Brush him! Check his feet for thorns! File his nails! His name is Sahib."

"Sahib?" The name struck Run-Run as a curiosity. He had only heard the word addressed to foreigner bosses. Was the animal named because he was like a foreign sahib, white and proud?

The mahout was rattling on. "And you will feed him sugarcane! Coconuts! The finest grain! The cleanest hay! And he loves peppermint!"

"The sweepings of old hay at half the price will have to do," Run-Run replied. "And where am I to get peppermint? Out of thin air?"

"Idiot!" shouted the mahout on behalf of the prince. "Hay sweepings! You do not feed a white elephant like a pig. Respect what I say!"

Run-Run cocked an experienced eye at the cloud of an elephant. "He has good tusks," he said. "Clearing tree stumps pays rich for fast work. Sahib will earn himself fine dinners."

"Are you both an idiot and a fool?" The palace mahout now broke open a laugh, displaying a junk heap of black and broken teeth. "Stumps! Nay, young worm! You may not work a white elephant! Do you think they were born to carry logs and clear fields like jungle beasts?"

"An elephant is an elephant," said Run-Run confidently. What nonsense was the man talking?

The mahout's voice raised itself to an impatient shout. "Mud head! White elephants are sacred!"

"Sacred? Like a holy man?"

"A gift from the heavens!"

"Truly?"

"Scrub him! Water him! Feed him generously! Do you hear?"

Run-Run whispered for none to hear. "I am deaf with hearing you." He bowed his head out of habit rather than respect.

"Wash the hair at his ears! Brush it! Use no harsh words. Do not scold him. Treat him like an honored guest! If you value your own skin, you will be a servant to Prince Noi's gift—this high-born white elephant. The prince will have his eye upon you, sharp as arrows!"

Run-Run raised an eyebrow. "And tell me, Great Mahout of Us All, how am I to feed him if he cannot work, this noble Sahib?"

The mahout in his red jacket again cracked open a black smile. "That is the prince's curse upon you!"

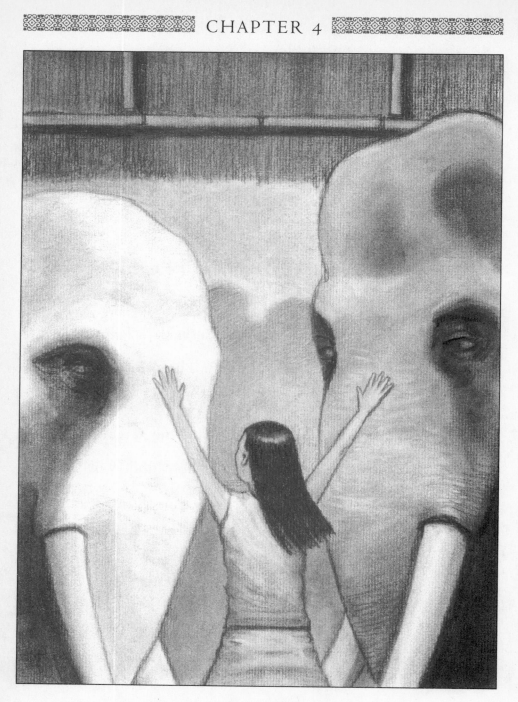

CHAPTER 4

Run-Run rose from his bed to push them apart.

Run-Run AND THE Runaway

That night Run-Run lay on the hay that would be tomorrow's breakfast for the two beasts. The elephants filled the log stable as snugly as two feet in one shoe. He had chained one of Sahib's hind feet to the stout teak picket driven deep into the ground by his grandfather long ago, when time began.

Walking Mountain regarded the new elephant with curiosity. When Sahib crowded him, there came a loud clacking of tusks. Run-Run rose from his bed to push them apart.

"Behave, Walking Mountain! Our guest is bad mannered. But give him extra room, eh?"

The old elephant rumbled and grumbled from the depths of his throat.

Even in the dark, Run-Run could tell the animals apart. Walking Mountain gave off an earthy smell. The white elephant carried about him the scent of lime blossoms and incense.

It was all too clear that Sahib had never labored, except to eat and drink. The animal's tusks hadn't a scratch on them. They looked as polished as glass.

But how curious Sahib was! Like a mongoose, Run-Run noticed. His trunk had already explored the thatch of the roof and the cracks between the logs. He boldly sniffed at Run-Run's small bundle of possessions. The boy knotted the cloth a second and third time.

In the middle of the night, Sahib began pulling at his leg chain. Run-Run thought about this for a while. Then, with a sudden and happy grin, he knew a way to put his unhappy burden at an end. Hadn't the black-toothed mahout said that the noble Sahib must be allowed to do as he pleased?

And wasn't it clear that the imperial guest now wanted his leg freed from the elephant chain?

Run-Run would be glad to oblige! And if the white elephant chose to run free as a jungle parrot, whose fault would that be?

The boy silently unlocked the leg chain. To the distant song of old Bangrak's wind chimes tinkling in his ears, he fell back to sleep. Smiling.

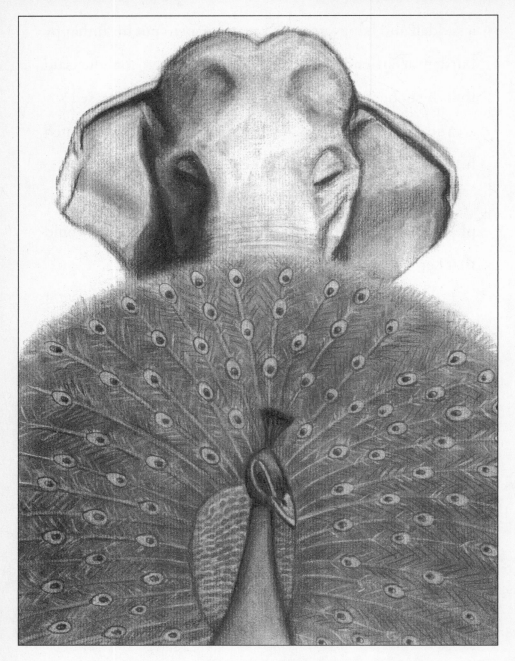

CHAPTER 5

He was heading upriver, curiously following a peacock.

Run-Run AND A Wave OF THE Hand

On his thick bed of hay in the elephant stable, Run-Run awoke with a sweaty sense that something was wrong. Was he seeing a ghost in the shadows?

Wrong, indeed! It was only Sahib, white as a spirit, asleep on his feet beside Walking Mountain.

"Rude guest! Why didn't you run away? Are you so pleased with my poor hospitality you chose to stay?"

The boy dismissed the matter with a scratch of

the head. He fed the animals, ate a bowl of rice with three dashes of hot sauce, and began the day's work. It was barely dawn.

He led Walking Mountain out of the stable and rode to the hillside plantation. Left behind and unshackled, the white elephant had all day to wander off, in command of his own life.

But at midday, when the boy and Walking Mountain returned to the stable, there inside stood Sahib, swaying contentedly. He had eaten the hay Run-Run had slept on and the juicy sections of sugarcane Run-Run had been saving for himself. Walking Mountain would never have been so rude and selfish!

Run-Run's temper ignited. But he remembered the warning: He must not shout at the sacred elephant. He could not scold his unwelcome guest.

Run-Run climbed up Sahib's trunk as he might a coconut tree. He seated himself and gave the beast a prod. At least the white elephant knew his commands. Leaving the stable behind, they lumbered down to the river. Grumpily, Walking Mountain followed along behind.

"Hear me, big brother!" Run-Run called back. "Do not be jealous. I must tend this white heap of an important being, but it is you I love!"

Sahib allowed himself to be washed and the tuft of his tail to be brushed out. He chirped as softly as wind chimes. He drank. He gurgled contentedly. He flapped his ears like great palm fans. Then he trumpeted to the world, loudly.

Walking Mountain looked on with mild scorn and then turned away. He gave a short but louder trumpet blast, as if to say such jungle tricks were nothing special. Anyone could flap his ears and trumpet to the sky.

Run-Run now checked Walking Mountain's feet for thorns and his toenails for bruises. He knew that an elephant's toenails were tender to the touch. He had seen mahouts punishing their beast by striking their toenails. Never had he treated Walking Mountain with such unkindness.

Out of the corner of his eye, Run-Run noticed the white elephant wandering off. He was heading upriver, curiously following a peacock. The bird strutted as proudly as Prince Noi himself, screaming from tree to tree and rattling open its huge sunrise of a tail.

Run-Run watched quietly. Would Sahib vanish around a bend and keep walking?

He might.

He did!

The boy smiled with all his teeth. He waved his hand.

"Farewell, white elephant," he muttered. "Good-bye, Sahib Pest!"

CHAPTER 6

Taking a few steps forward, Sahib dug his polished ivory tusks around a dried stump.

Dangerous Mischief

Two days later, the morning sun rose hot to the touch. The mud plastered over Walking Mountain's hide had curled and was dropping like a fall of leaves. Well before noon, Run-Run gave his elephant a tap. "Enough, beloved! Let us not melt like temple candles! Catch your breath, magnificent one."

Resting for the first time in hours, Run-Run was startled to look over and see Sahib standing out in the sun with crows landing on his shoulders. "Pest! So you are back, runaway beast! No one to wash your tail or fetch for you? What are you gazing at? Walking Mountain at hard work to feed you?"

The white elephant flapped buzz flies from his ears, startling the crows into flight.

Run-Run was careful to keep his voice polite so as not to offend by his tone. "Do you see any shade here in the ill-tempered fields? Even the flies are falling dead in midair. And if you fall to your knees with heatstroke? Who will the prince blame? He'll shout, 'Bring me that elephant brat!' "

Run-Run wiped his forehead with his bare arm. "So! Be so kind as to run away again. Kindly vanish!"

The sacred elephant ignored the boy's earnest suggestion. Taking a few steps forward, Sahib dug his polished ivory tusks around a dried stump. Pushing with his forehead, he lifted the root out of the earth and flung it aside. Just as he had seen Walking Mountain do.

Run-Run gave the beast a forbidden shout. "Wicked

rascal! Have you no kindness? If the prince discovers you plucking trees, he will twist my head from my shoulders like a chicken!"

The white elephant ignored him and, using his tusks as skillfully as the white man's fork, lifted another stump.

Run-Run gave out a great groan. He looked around at the mahouts at work clearing nearby fields. Had anyone caught sight of the white elephant's daring mischief?

He saw a thin-chested mahout pointing a finger like a dried twig. Run-Run recognized him as the neighbor everyone called Fish Eyes.

Run-Run climbed onto Sahib's neck. Where to hide? Where? Hardly a plantation tree was left standing! But there lingered the hot sun, still low enough to blaze into everyone's eyes.

Run-Run quickly prodded the white elephant to turn around and stride toward the morning sun. Let Fish Eyes gaze all he wished! Let Fish Eyes blind himself!

CHAPTER 7

"A cheeky scrap of nothing, you are!" said Fish Eyes.

Run-Run AND Fish Eyes

The next day, to keep the white elephant from further mischief, Run-Run again chained Sahib's rear foot to the stable's teak post. At the plantation he had bought a broken load of partly soured hay, the best he could afford for his two animals. He picked out and burned the spoilage. While the animals made crackling sounds at their breakfast, he fixed himself a rice cake in the ashes of his fire.

And there stood the mahout Fish Eyes. He was a long, bony man with sweeping mustaches as stained as drainpipes under his nostrils. He claimed the power to tell your future, for a coin or two, by reading a toss of dog bones. It was said that, so cunning was the mahout, that he could plant weeds and harvest rice.

"So the prince has blessed you with a white elephant," he remarked, snickering broadly.

"I am a lucky one, eh sir?" replied Run-Run, thinking it better to thicken his skin for this conversation. "Imagine! A dung beetle like me with two great elephants! Surely, the world is jealous."

"Spare me such good fortune!" replied the mahout. "Boy, does the prince know I saw you working the white elephant in the field?"

"Does the prince tell me what he knows?" Run-Run replied. "Do I tell the prince what I know?"

"You worked a sacred elephant," Fish Eyes said, no longer snickering. His eyes, sparking like flints, bore into Run-Run.

"With respects, perhaps you are mistaken," said Run-Run, beginning to eat. What could this bony nuisance of a man be after?

"With respects, my two eyes saw you."

"The sun was in your two eyes," Run-Run remarked simply. He would confess nothing to this man. "The white elephant may have enjoyed scratching his forehead against a stump when my back was turned. To scratch an itch is not work, venerable mahout."

The man brushed aside his mustaches and leaned forward. "What do you suppose the prince would pay to learn that you are thumbing your nose at him, eh? And mistreating the noble elephant?"

"The next time you see such nonsense, put spectacles on your nose!"

"A cheeky scrap of nothing, you are!" said Fish Eyes.

"I mistreat nothing, sir." Run-Run was not going to be frightened by this troublemaking mahout. "And you, sir?

All the world can see the sores on your elephant's trunk. A kind master would rest him to heal."

"Mind your own business, maggot!"

"Kindly set me the example," Run-Run snapped back, surprised at his own boldness.

Fish Eyes rose. He chose to smile, deepening the creases in his face, and swaggered off.

Run-Run finished his meal silently, his appetite knotted up inside his stomach. He must not allow the white elephant to work in the fields again.

He watered his animals and found a small thorn in Sahib's foot. The elephant showed no gratitude, except to spray Run-Run with water.

The next morning, the boy took extra care with Sahib's leg irons. He wound up the chain short and firm. Before leaving the stable, he checked again. "Stay, Sahib!" he commanded.

The white elephant trumpeted in protest, as out of sorts as a child left behind.

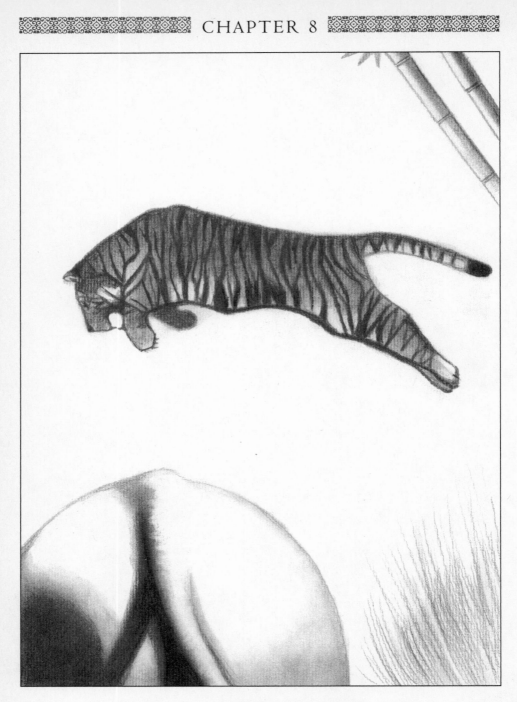

CHAPTER 8

The great cat leaped onto the white elephant's back.

At the River

Run-Run could not believe his eyes! Was he having visions in the heat shimmering over the fields?

There came the white elephant, swaggering and as free as a cloud. He hadn't escaped the leg chain. He had worked the teak stake out of the ground and was now dragging it behind him like an anchor.

The beast gazed with his huge and curious eyes at every move Walking Mountain was making. He turned and approached a dead jackfruit stump. Swinging his tufted tail, he uplifted the root as twisted as a tangle of snakes.

"Devil!" the boy whispered, fearful of uttering a curse of greater fury. "Behaving like a beast for hire! Perhaps the prince will take pity and merely skin me from my bones, eh? And where have you been? You are crawling like a tree with red ants."

Run-Run wasted no time leading the white elephant to the river. He worked the leg chain loose. After scrubbing Sahib of ants, he prodded him to the mud wallow and a good roll in the mud.

When Sahib had had enough and began to find his feet, Run-Run's breath caught like a bone in his throat. He peered and then blinked at the sight of his white cloud of an elephant rising from the mud. Sahib's hide had turned red.

"Oh, royal pest!" Run-Run declared with breathless amusement. "Have you rusted like an iron pot? Not even the great prince would know you!"

Run-Run's amusement turned to growing delight. He gazed at the red elephant and thought: What was there now to fear? For all to see, he commanded a work elephant shimmering with mud. He snapped his fingers like a bazaar magician. The white elephant had vanished in a puff of air.

The next day, Run-Run allowed the muddy elephant to amuse himself plowing up tree stumps. "How eager you are to try out your tusks!" he called. "Have your days been so boring in the prince's stable, eh? Nothing to do but to stand and be brushed and admired like a peacock in a cage?"

When Run-Run caught sight of the meddlesome mahout across the fields, he smiled openly. What could Fish Eyes see with his crafty eyes? Nothing but another tusker covered with red mud.

Later, Run-Run found a spot in the river, free of the other mahouts, to water and replaster his elephant with mud.

"Don't you look beautiful!" he declared, giving Sahib an affectionate pat. "Tonight your earnings will provide a dinner of sugarcane and two stalks of bananas! And coconuts, why not, to chew like peanuts in the shell?"

Nearby, Walking Mountain rose from the water, ears wide and quickly alert.

As suddenly as a flash of summer lightning, a tiger broke from the trees. Run-Run saw a streak of yellow through the air. The great cat leaped onto the white elephant's back. Was that tiger crazy, to attack an elephant? His claws dug in, and Sahib let out an astonished bellow.

Run-Run saw that Sahib was not trained to protect himself! Was that left to gun bearers? The white elephant dropped to a knee. Run-Run picked up a river rock to throw.

He saw Walking Mountain's ears flaring. Jungle smart and trumpeting, the old elephant rushed forward. He knocked Sahib around and off his legs. The tiger bounded to the riverbank and swiftly turned for another attack.

Walking Mountain thundered forward, his great tusks

swinging. He skewered the tiger. With a mighty toss of his head, the old elephant flung the tiger into the air like a discarded toy. Gored and bleeding, the tiger gave a furious cry and fled back into the trees.

Run-Run had seen two ears. This was not the murdering old tiger he'd hoped to meet someday. He rushed through the river shadows to comfort his white elephant. And then he turned to old Walking Mountain and hugged his trunk. "You are brave, great brother! How I love you!"

CHAPTER 9

He talked all the while, closely, softly, to comfort the injured animal.

Tiger Claws

Old Walking Mountain couldn't do the work of two, but he tried. Run-Run was almost too busy to eat. For days, he washed the white Sahib's injuries with fresh water. He used his elephant file to make charcoal powder. Mixing it with the clearest mud he could find, he made poultices to slap over the wounds. Two and three times a day he refreshed the charcoal and mud. He talked all the while, closely, softly, to comfort the injured animal.

"How fine you look, eh?" he muttered, petting

the elephant. "See how you heal? But listen to me, Sahib. You must have eyes in the back of your head for murderers. You have tusks to protect yourself. Better than rifles, your tusks! Did you see Walking Mountain? Did you pay attention? Remember when you were a baby and tried to lap water with your lips like a pariah dog? Someone had to teach you to use your trunk, to blow a waterfall down your throat. Your tusks, too, must learn to protect you."

He threw an arm around Sahib's trunk and gave a hug. "How jealous the plantation mahouts must be to see an elephant brat like me with two handsome beasts! Let them think what they like!"

In the small stable at night, Run-Run saw Sahib rub his side against Walking Mountain, as if to find comfort in the old elephant's presence.

"I think he is beginning to admire you, big brother," Run-Run remarked in the morning. "Give him a honk. Give him a chirp."

But while Walking Mountain tolerated his stablemate, he gave no sign that he was prepared to become friends.

Weeks later, with the tiger wounds healing well, Run-Run was awakened from his sleep. The tip of an elephant's trunk was sniffing his nose, his mouth, his ears, and touching his neck. He thought it must be Walking Mountain showing his old affection.

He rose to an elbow and pushed away the trunk. That's when he saw that it was Sahib. Sahib, who now smelled of the earth.

CHAPTER 10

Run-Run caught sight of Prince Noi not far off on his hunting elephant.

Sahib in Danger

The rumor had spread from village to village that a white elephant could be seen and, perhaps, even touched. The visitors would bring gifts of banana stalks and frangipani blossoms and even a hoarded coin or two.

Run-Run did not welcome these intruders. Sahib was well and eager to be out and about and working with his mahout in the fields. Still unaware of his great strength, he was apt to give Run-Run a nudge of affection, knocking the boy into the dirt.

"Big cousin!" Run-Run would say, laughing. "I beg you to remember I am not an elephant!"

The hot season was ending, and the days were pleasant. One day shabby clouds came sweeping across the sky. Run-Run and Sahib were clearing stumps. Walking Mountain had begun to limp in the mornings and did little but watch.

Run-Run caught sight of Prince Noi not far off on his hunting elephant. He patted Sahib as if to comfort himself. Let the prince look over as the road led the hunting party closer. He would see only a mahout and two work elephants covered with red mud.

And then the breeze shifted. Winds from the teak forests in the north slid across Run-Run's face. Dark clouds as full as water buckets rushed overhead. Within moments the boy and his elephants were standing in a downpour.

Run-Run's breath caught. Sahib was turning white as a cloud! The prince would be certain to notice.

Run-Run looked for a place to hide. There wasn't a tree left standing.

But there stood Walking Mountain.

Run-Run ran up Sahib's trunk. Seated on the elephant's neck, he called out sharp commands.

"Turn! This way! This way!"

Sahib, his tusks in the earth, was following his own commands. His tusks got a good grip on a jackfruit root.

"Drop it! Turn! Do as I say! Quick!"

Run-Run gave the white elephant a couple of kicks under the ears. He was aware that the road was bringing the prince closer by the moment.

"Listen! Sahib! If you love me, you will turn sharply. You will stand beside Walking Mountain. Please, closer than a shadow!"

Now Sahib lifted his head as if to peer at the noisy mahout on his neck. Then he gave a heavy blow through his trunk and moved. He turned. He rubbed his side against Walking

Mountain's and stopped, largely hidden. Run-Run gave him a pat.

"Ten thousand blessings on you, elephant of elephants."

Run-Run was sure that the prince had given them a long glance. There was no white-as-a-cloud elephant in plain sight. Then the summer shower of rain sent the hunting party back along the road to the palace.

"Why stand here in the rain, eh, Sahib? Come, Walking Mountain. Home. And let me have a look at your hurting leg."

It seemed an eternity before Run-Run's heart stopped drumming.

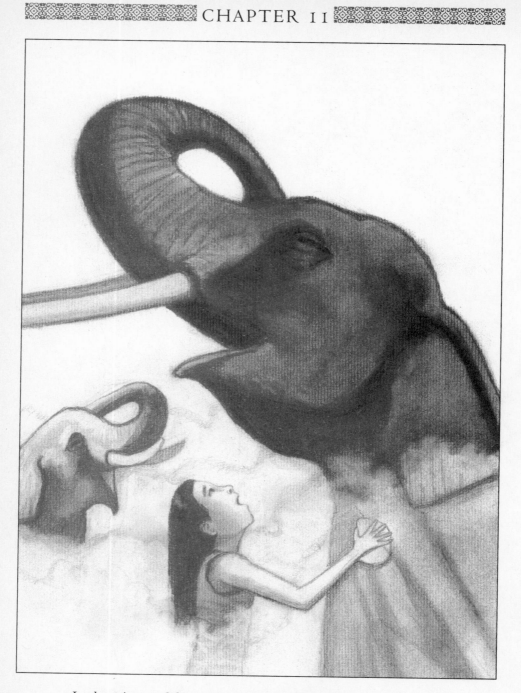

CHAPTER 11

In the privacy of the stable, he hand-rubbed Walking Mountain
with flour until he looked white.

Rice Flour

Out of the rain under the stable roof, Run-Run had a close look at Walking Mountain's morning limp. There were no thorns or split toenails this time. Perhaps it was only old age announcing itself. And look at his four teeth, grown so big! He had outgrown five earlier sets of molars, and these were the last he could expect. Once they fell out, he'd no longer be able to chew. He would slowly starve and die before Run-Run's weepy eyes. It was the way of elephants.

When the roads dried, Run-Run felt emboldened enough to take Sahib, mudded over, back into the fields. But what of the neighboring villagers who still came to see the white elephant and would find the stable empty? Would they guess that Run-Run was working the noble beast?

Run-Run slapped his hands together. He knew exactly what to do. At the plantation warehouse, he traded his elephant's labors for a heavy sack of rice flour. In the privacy of the stable, he hand-rubbed Walking Mountain with flour until he looked white. Not as white as Sahib, but close enough.

During the following days, Run-Run allowed Walking Mountain to remain behind in the comfort and shadows of the stable. Let anyone come and look, even the prince's men. They'd need torches to tell the difference.

While Run-Run and Sahib worked in the fields, wise old Bangrak realized what the boy had done and put himself in charge of the stable. Within a few days, he confessed his happy mischief. He had collected several bronze coins and one silver from those curious to see the famous white elephant.

"But it is only Walking Mountain!" Run-Run protested when he learned what old Bangrak had done.

"And are you not working the white elephant. Eh? True? But look how your old elephant enjoys the attention and the bananas and the frangipani flowers to wear around his neck. And some come hoping a touch of the white elephant will cure them of backache and runny noses. So everyone is content!"

"But we are cheating!"

"Doesn't everyone cheat the ignorant? It makes them so happy!"

Was this true, Run-Run wondered? Was he to be equal only to crafty men like Fish Eyes? "No," he said. "Turn everyone away from my rice-powdered elephant. Sahib works fast, and we will be able to provide Walking Mountain all the bananas and frangipanis he wishes."

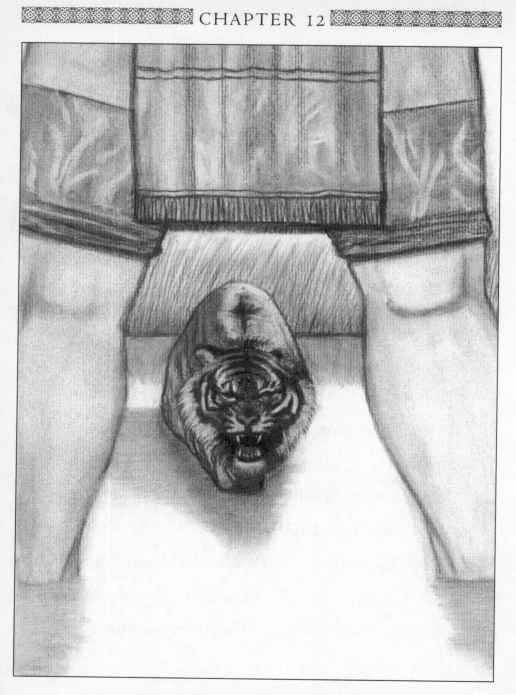

CHAPTER 12

Without a weapon he was facing death.

The Attack

Run-Run was ready when the dry season finally blew away and the monsoon rains came with a roar. He stored hay and grain and sugarcane to the leafy roof of the stable. Day by day, the dark skies blew wet and rowdy until only a fish could plod along the roads. The visitors stopped coming to see Run-Run's white elephant.

On the worst days, the boy and his animals confined themselves to the stable, with plenty to eat. When Run-Run looked at how well Sahib's tiger wounds had healed, he felt a certain pride. Could he learn more and one day have a certificate to show how clever he was? After all, old Bangrak had sent his son away to school and to poke his nose into the world beyond the teak mountains.

Run-Run wondered what a school looked like. He'd heard of the world, too, but couldn't imagine anyplace so full of people. But why dream about such things? His teeth would grow old, like Walking Mountain's. He would go lame and spend his last days still sleeping on a pile of hay. All was clear to see. It was the fate of Run-Run to be Run-Run, the mahout.

It seemed weeks before the sun boldly returned and, like a wizard's trick, dried up the muddy roads and fields. Soon Run-Run and Sahib were back at their occupation. But always the boy's eye was on the sky, for the monsoon season was long and roguish.

One midday Run-Run was scrubbing Sahib clean in the river and examining him for small cuts and bruises. The blare of a hunting trumpet froze him to the spot. The prince was approaching! And there stood Sahib, a work elephant, bare and white as chalk!

There was no place to run. There was no place to hide, for bursting from the trees came Prince Noi. He rode alone in the wicker howdah while his mahout sat on the neck of his hunting elephant. They began crossing the river.

Run-Run froze. He felt caught. Didn't the prince have anything to do with his days but hunt beasts?

The mahout in his blazing red coat already had Run-Run pinned down with his raven's eyes. He stopped in the center of the narrow river. "There! You, boy! What have you been up to? Do you see him, Excellency? The white elephant has been abused! Look at his forehead! His tusks! They are the scratches of field labor!"

The prince scowled. "So! So, elephant brat, you have disobeyed me."

"No, fine Excellency," said Run-Run. "Sahib commands

himself. I but followed his own wishes. It amuses him to pull stumps and carry logs!"

"Amuses!"

"Allow me to show you."

"I am hunting tigers. I have no time for insolent stories." Prince Noi picked up a rifle. "You have legs. Run, boy! It will amuse me to hunt you like a tiger. Run! You may be quick-witted enough to escape!"

"No, kind prince," said Run-Run. "I was not born to be hunted like jungle game."

Run-Run was surprised by his own fit of dignity. He saw rifles stored in the howdah like chopsticks. Was there time to tell Sahib that he had come to love him like Walking Mountain? Yes, before the prince's foolish temper ended Run-Run's insignificant life?

He was sufficiently distracted by these thoughts that he failed to become aware of Sahib's ears. They swung forward, flaring in alarm. But when the elephant lifted its trunk to trumpet, Run-Run awoke to the rush of danger. He stiffened.

A tiger? Another?

Yes, a yellow tiger!

Run-Run saw it, bursting out of the trees as if through breaking glass.

He stiffened. Hadn't a tiger more sense than to attack a huge and dangerous elephant?

The animal made a powerful leap, his glare attaching itself to the prince. Was he remembering the tiger hunter from some past encounter? The wicker howdah overturned.

Thrown into midair, Prince Noi discharged his rifle as it fell from his hands. He missed everything but the Siamese sky.

The tiger recovered his legs. The prince, too, was now on his legs. Without a weapon he was facing death.

The tiger sprang.

In that split second Run-Run saw that the big cat had lost

an ear. The left ear! There, before his eyes, leaped the murderer who had tried to drag off his mother.

Run-Run felt Sahib's silver ankus in his fist. He heaved it at the tiger.

CHAPTER 13

The white elephant was trumpeting to shatter the sky.

Sahib's Fate

The white elephant was trumpeting to shatter the sky. Had he taken Run-Run's flight of the prod as a command to charge? When Run-Run looked up again, he saw Sahib thundering forward.

The tiger made a quick change of direction and might have leaped safely into the lower limbs of the trees. But he failed to clear the advancing tusks, sharp as crescent moons.

With a great toss of his head, as he had watched Walking Mountain do, Sahib pitched the tiger into the air. When the bleeding cat found his feet, Sahib gored him again.

Now there was a shot in the air as the mahout picked up the rifle and finished off the beast. From the tiger's first leap to Sahib's triumphant blast, the moments had followed one another in a long breath. Run-Run's heart was still racing up in his throat.

Sahib returned to the boy's side, almost pushing him over. Run-Run wrapped his arms around his white trunk and caught a look from the prince.

"Elephant boy," said the monarch, "young mahout! You have trained your animal well."

"He learns quickly."

"You and the white elephant have saved your prince from a few tiger scratches. I shall reward you."

A few scratches? Your life, Prince Noi the Idle! Run-Run said nothing aloud.

"I shall remove the curse from you. I shall take back the white elephant."

Run-Run gazed hard at the prince. "It will not honor me to return a gift."

"I will send a mahout for him."

Then he tossed Run-Run a pouch jingling with coins.

CHAPTER 14

Then he turned away, without a word and without a final wave of the hand.

Run-Run Waits

Run-Run took no interest in emptying the pouch and counting the coins. He threw it in a corner of the stable like something despised. It was as if the prince were buying back the white elephant.

Run-Run slept badly.

Sahib sensed his mahout's wounded spirit. At the riverbank, he wrapped his trunk around Run-Run's legs. The boy pulled himself free. "No, Sahib! I don't feel like playing."

Moments later, returning to the stable,

Run-Run felt the elephant's trunk at his back. Sahib gave the boy a mischievous push. Run-Run was knocked over as easily as a fence post. He picked himself up and gave Sahib a look. But he said nothing.

Sahib lowered his trunk and playfully shoved him again—and again.

"Enough!" Run-Run called out.

But Sahib wouldn't stop. Again and again Sahib's trunk nudged him until the boy couldn't hold back a grin. "Sahib. I told you. Don't bother me with games!"

But again, there came Sahib's playful trunk. Despite himself, Run-Run began to laugh. He clutched his knees while Sahib rolled him like a ball back to the riverbank and prankishly into the water. Run-Run took a gulp of water and spit it out like a stream of sparks in the sun. The sound of his own laughter had surprised him. Now Sahib spread his front legs and gave a satisfied blast of his trumpet.

And the boy said aloud to the flapping of Sahib's ears,

"When you are gone, you must not push the prince. Do you understand, beloved? You must behave!"

The next morning, Run-Run was relieved to notice that Walking Mountain's limp disappeared as the sun rose above the treetops. Was it just a morning stiffness of the old?

The boy scrubbed Sahib as clean as when the animal had first arrived. He filed the pads of his feet. He wanted to be sure that the palace mahouts would have no contempt for Run-Run's care.

He washed his own ears and his long hair, and gave it a swing around his neck like a wet towel.

Then he sat on his heels at the stable and waited. His eyes could not ignore the road. At any moment, a mahout would appear to lead Sahib away.

Walking Mountain couldn't know that his stablemate would soon be gone, but he behaved as if he sensed a bad change in the weather. He made uneasy, soft guttural sounds.

When the palace mahout arrived at midday, Run-Run waited a moment and then rose to his feet. Without a word, he unshackled the white elephant.

"The silver prod, boy."

When he handed it over, the mahout was commanding Sahib to kneel so that he could mount to the beast's neck.

The white elephant had become accustomed to Run-Run's voice. He ignored the mahout's command.

With a flash of impatience, the mahout turned to Run-Run. "Tell him to kneel and let's be done with this!"

The boy glared at the mahout. Wasn't it enough that the man was taking Sahib away? Was Run-Run obliged to help?

With first tears rising to his eyes, the boy gave the command, and Sahib kneeled. The prince's mahout climbed to his place and gave the elephant a sharp rap with the ankus. "Go!"

Run-Run didn't want Sahib beaten with the prod. He tried to clear his throat. "Do what he says, beloved Sahib. Go."

The great elephant moved forward. Run-Run watched for a moment, his eyes swimming. There was no one to see the tears but Walking Mountain. Run-Run wrapped an arm around the old elephant's trunk. Then he turned away, without a word and without a final wave of the hand.

That night he slept curled up between Walking Mountain's front legs. There he felt safe from the world.

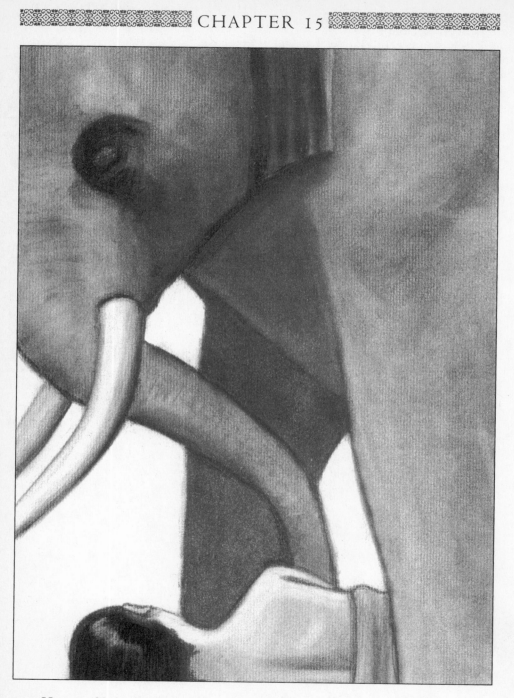

CHAPTER 15

How could this be Walking Mountain, smelling of blossoms and incense?

Run-Run Awakens

The monsoon rains returned with howling snorts and the clatter of fallen trees. Run-Run ventured out only when the wet winds tired of Chattershee and whisked themselves away.

The boy had fallen silent as stone. He parted his lips only to mutter a command to Walking Mountain. He hadn't a word to say aloud when he heard that Fish Eyes had been banished weeks before from the Siamese hillsides.

The cunning mahout had ridden to the palace.

Confidently he had offered his hand to invite a reward for spying on the boy mahout, Run-Run. The white elephant, said he, was clearly put to work at forbidden labor.

"Was the sun in your eyes?" The prince had exploded. "The white elephant is in my stable!"

Fish Eyes hadn't heard.

The king had folded his arms as tight as a knot. "What kind of spying is this? You cannot plant weeds and harvest rice! Liar! You are banished!"

When old Bangrak brought him the news, Run-Run shrugged and walked away. What did it matter if Fish Eyes had set a mousetrap and caught himself? Run-Run chose not to be freshly reminded of his days riding as happy as a songbird on Sahib's broad neck.

Once again the roads were drying out, leaving rain puddles as bright as broken mirrors. The silent boy returned with Walking Mountain to their plantation labors. Despite himself, Run-Run couldn't keep flashes of handsome Sahib from intruding across his mind. The elephant must be again accustomed to being served like a sacred guest. He would soon forget Run-Run and Walking Mountain.

One night, Run-Run awoke with Walking Mountain's trunk at his ear and neck. The boy pushed the animal away and turned over to sleep again.

But there again came the trunk sniffing him. Run-Run rose to an elbow. "Don't be a pest, big brother! It's not time to get up!"

Once more, Run-Run turned over. Once more the elephant trunk was a nuisance at his ear.

The boy lay there. A question rose in a flash. How could this be Walking Mountain, smelling of blossoms and incense?

Run-Run sat up sharply.

Sahib? Impossible!

The boy peered into the darkness. Was that a moon cloud beside him?

"Sahib!"

He leaped to his feet and clutched that great white trunk. "Look, do you see, big brother? It is Sahib!"

Walking Mountain had already swung his head and was rubbing his side against his old stablemate. He began to chatter deep in his throat.

When Run-Run backed off to gaze at the visitor, he said in an amazed whisper, "What are you doing here? Shall I guess? Have you run away?"

Run-Run didn't know his eyes were full of tears until he had to wipe them.

"Would you like a piece of sugarcane, eh? So you have come home to us!"

Now Run-Run gave his nose a big wipe. Was there ever a nose in all Siam to be so wet?

He fed each elephant chunks of sugarcane out of his hands.

Was this a punishment, to be so happy? he wondered

sharply. A shadow was falling across his mind. How can I keep the prince's white elephant? Sahib has only declared himself a holiday. I must return him.

Yes, I must.

Indeed, I must.

But if I don't?

You are not a prince, to do as you please.

But what of Sahib? He, too, may do as he pleases.

True.

A white elephant must be obeyed.

Mustn't the prince, also, be obeyed?

True.

And he will be furious.

But isn't the prince always furious?

Wipe your nose.

I am.

Well?

I am thinking.

So?

I think I must disobey the prince.

And obey the white elephant?

It is settled.

Look. See how happy Sahib looks?

I see!

And the prince will look as if he choked on a fish bone!

CHAPTER 16

"Bring us luck, white elephant!"

The Vagabonds

"Ten thousand pardons, prince," Run-Run said aloud, as if saying lines in a bazaar shadow play. "You declared that the white elephant commands his own life. He must be obeyed in his every wish. And isn't it clear that he wishes to belong to Run-Run, not to you, excellent prince?" And then the boy added softly, "May you not choke on a fish bone!"

The sun was rising, like a bloodshot eye. The boy unshackled Walking Mountain and watered the two elephants. Then, with quick decision, he covered the white elephant with red mud.

"We must go," he declared, smiling with confidence. Walking Mountain's limp might slow them down, but only during the raw mornings. There would be tons of food to browse once they reached the teak mountains.

They returned to the stable for Run-Run's bundle of possessions. He slipped his grandfather's porcelain amulet around his neck. He cocked his father's colored headdress on his head.

He gave the stable a last look for anything he might have forgotten. There, hiding like a mouse under the corner straw, lay the prince's pouch of coins. Run-Run picked it up.

Prince Noi had tossed it as a reward for saving his idle life. It was a true gift, was it not?

Run-Run unknotted the drawstring and shook coins onto his palm. He held out the money for his elephants to see. "Look! A fortune in silver!" he exclaimed.

He turned his back on the stable that had been his home

for so long. He climbed onto the neck of Walking Mountain. The old elephant would set the pace. Sahib, his hide mud stained, would follow.

Follow where? The other side of the far mountains had always beckoned Run-Run. What would he find?

Hadn't his father always complained that in Chattershee everyone lived under a coconut shell? Run-Run was aware of a moment's fear, to be tumbling outside the safety of the shell. Were there serpents and dragons out there?

But there must be a school. He had enough silver for that!

He turned for a last look at the village houses standing huddled in the dawn shadows. He could hear the faint stirring of old Bangrak's wind chimes.

"Good-bye, Chattershee," he said.

Before long, the village vanished behind him. He gave Walking Mountain a reassuring pat. And then he threw a smile at Sahib, in full sway behind him.

"Bring us luck, white elephant!"

Author's Note

While this story is a work of imagination, it was inspired by a curious event half a world away and centuries ago.

Before old Siam gave itself a new name, Thailand, a great king became angry at one of his palace advisers. With a mad twinkle in his eye, King Rama gave the courtier a white elephant. That would punish the man! Regarded as sacred, the royal beast was not allowed to work. Nevertheless, the white elephant must be fed its hundreds of pounds of fruit and fodder a day and otherwise cared for. The courtier was ruined.

The term survives today in white elephant sales, during which unwanted or burdensome objects are offered for sale. The old king would be amused.